Hanukkah

Story and pictures by Miriam Nerlove

ALBERT WHITMAN & COMPANY, MORTON GROVE, ILLINOIS

For Abe and Alana, with love.

Special thanks to Cantor Howard Tushman and
Rabbi Joseph A. Edelheit, Congregation Emanuel, Chicago.

Text and Illustrations © 1989 by Miriam Nerlove.
Published in 1989 by Albert Whitman & Company,
6340 Oakton Street, Morton Grove, Illinois 60053.
Published simultaneously in Canada by
General Publishing, Limited, Toronto.
Printed in the United States of America.
10   9   8   7   6   5   4

Library of Congress Cataloging-in-Publication Data

Nerlove, Miriam.
Hanukkah/written and illustrated by Miriam Nerlove.
p.   cm.
Summary: Rhyming text and illustrations follow the activities
of a little boy and his parents as they prepare to celebrate
Hanukkah.
ISBN 0-8075-3143-X (lib. bdg.)
ISBN 0-8075-3142-1 (pbk.)
[1. Hanukkah—Fiction. 2. Stories in rhyme.] I. Title.
PZ8.3.N365Han   1989   88-36648
[E]—dc19   CIP
                                                    AC

HANUKKAH! Hanukkah's finally here!
For eight nights we celebrate each year.

Let's read the story of how it began…
Once Antiochus, the king of the land,
took the Jews' Temple and gave his command.

"You may not worship your One God," he said.
"You must worship my gods, in my way, instead!"

So first Mattathias, then Judah, his son,

led their Maccabee army and fought till they won.

They took back their Temple and kindled a light

with just enough oil to burn for one night.

But a miracle happened! The light burned for eight!
That's why today we still celebrate.

Let's find the menorah and polish it bright.

We'll add one more candle
each Hanukkah night

with the shammash,
the candle that lights other lights.

Each night in the window, the candles will glow.
We celebrate freedom—let everyone know!

Some nights we fry latkes—Dad makes them so well.
They're ready to eat. What a wonderful smell!

Sufganiyot are doughnuts Mom serves after dinner.
They come in all sizes, some thicker, some thinner.

We like to play dreidel and watch the top spin.
Which side will it fall on? Nun, gimel, hay, shin?

Nun means you get nothing...

Gimel, you win!

Each night there are gifts. Let's unwrap them and see
what wonderful fun trading presents can be!

Here is some Hanukkah gelt just for you.
It's money to save, but you spend a bit, too.

Grandpa and Grandma sing songs that they know,
the same ones they taught to your dad long ago.

The last candle's lit, and the last night is here.
Hanukkah's over—but just for this year.

One year from now—if we can just wait—
all over the world we'll again celebrate!

ANTIOCHUS	The Hellenistic king of Syria who outlawed Judaism and led armies against the Jewish people from 168 to 165 B.C.E. (B.C.).
DREIDEL	A top with Hebrew letters used in a popular Hanukkah game. Depending on whether the dreidel lands on *nun* (take nothing); *gimel* (take all); *hay* (take half); or *shin* (put something in), nuts or pennies are put in or removed from the "pot."
GELT	The word for "money" in Yiddish, a synthesis of German, Hebrew, and other languages that is spoken by some Jews of eastern and central European descent.
HANUKKAH	A Hebrew word for "dedication." The eight-day festival begins on the twenty-fifth day of the Hebrew month of Kislev (usually December). It celebrates the Maccabees' struggle for religious freedom, which culminated in the rededication of the Temple in Jerusalem.
LATKE	A word for "pancake" in Yiddish. On Hanukkah it is customary to eat potato latkes and other foods fried in oil. These bring to mind the miracle of the small jar of oil that burned for eight days in the Temple lamp.
MACCABEE	A Hebrew word for "hammer." About 167 B.C.E., Mattathias and his five sons formed an army known as the Maccabees to fight the forces of Antiochus. After Mattathias' death, his son Judah continued the struggle.
MENORAH	The seven-branched lamp which from ancient to modern times has served as the symbol of Israel. The Hanukkah menorah (*hanukkiah*) has nine branches, one for each night's candle and one for the shammash.
SHAMMASH	A Hebrew word for "servant." During Hanukkah, the shammash candle is lit first and then used to light the other candles.
SUFGANIYAH, SUFGANIYOT (plural)	A Hebrew word for "doughnut." Plain or jelly-filled, these fried doughnuts sprinkled with powdered sugar are served during Hanukkah.
TEMPLE	A building where Jews worship God. Judah and the Maccabees reclaimed the Temple in Jerusalem from the forces of Antiochus in 165 B.C.E. and restored and rededicated the building.